P9-BZX-586

# FIVE-MINUTE
# STORIES
## FOR
# GIRLS

hinkler

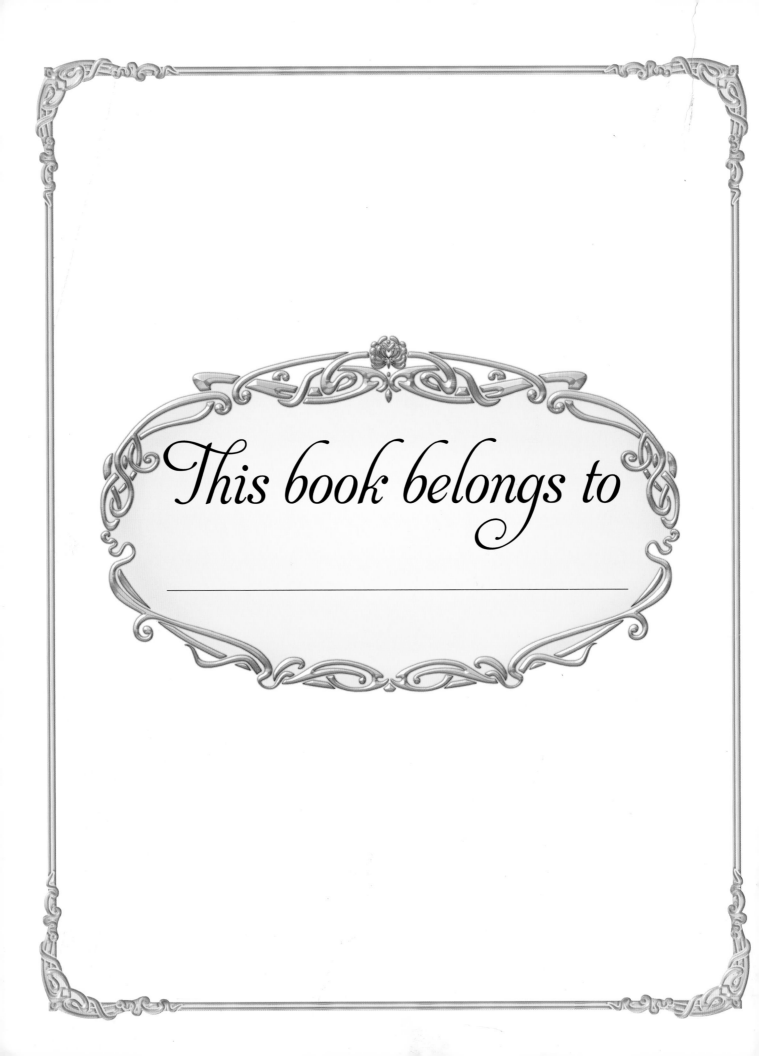

This book belongs to

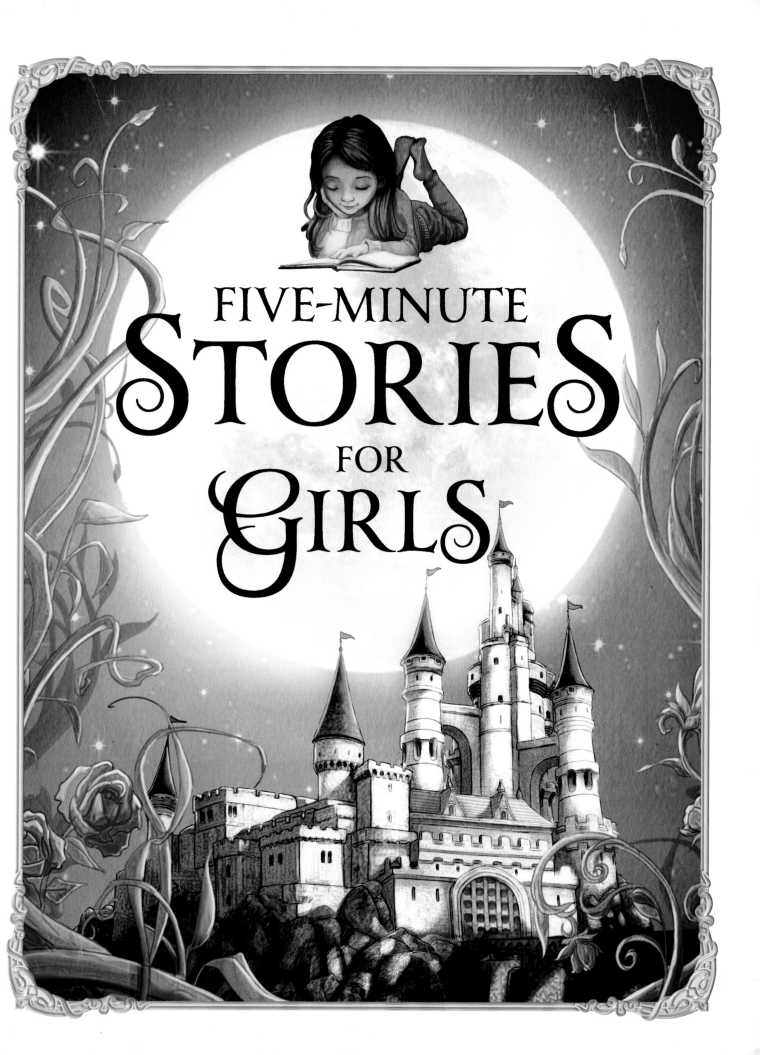

# FIVE-MINUTE
# STORIES
## FOR
# GIRLS

# h
## hinkler

Published by Hinkler Books Pty Ltd
45–55 Fairchild Street
Heatherton Victoria 3202 Australia
www.hinkler.com.au

© Hinkler Books Pty Ltd 2010, 2013

Cover Illustration: Adam Relf
Illustrators: Brijbasi Art Press Ltd
Editor: Suzannah Pearce
Designers: Diana Vlad, Mandi Cole and Ruth Comey
Prepress: Graphic Print Group

All rights reserved. No part of this publication may be reproduced, stored
in a retrieval system, or transmitted in any way or by any means, electronic,
mechanical, photocopying, recording or otherwise, without the prior written
permission of Hinkler Books Pty Ltd.

ISBN: 978 1 7435 2048 2

Printed and bound in China

# Contents

Introduction 6

Goldilocks and the Three Bears 7

The Princess and the Pea 17

Little Red Riding Hood 27

Thumbelina 37

The Little Red Hen 47

Rapunzel 57

The Shepherdess and the Chimney Sweep 67

The Wild Swans 77

The Little Match Girl 87

# Introduction

For centuries, fairytales have given children their first taste of the world of books and literature. Not only are folk and fairytales rollicking good fun, whisking children away to worlds of magic and imagination, they also teach valuable lessons about how to make your way in a world that can be dark and challenging.

Our favourite fairytale characters don't always have an easy time. They meet and overcome obstacles at every turn, just as our children will – though, hopefully, not in the form of wicked witches or mischievous goblins.

Among the best-known collectors of European folklore and mythology were Jacob and Wilhelm Grimm, from Germany, and Hans Christian Andersen, from Denmark. Not only did they collect and publish fairytales that had been passed on through oral tradition for centuries, but Andersen, in particular, created original tales of his own. Several of these works are featured in this book.

A key feature of many fairytales is brevity, their authors aiming to encapsulate timeless lessons on life in short, sharp, memorable style. As the title suggests, the stories in *Five-Minute Stories for Girls* are intended to be read in around five minutes, and are great for the short attention spans of young children or busy parents. The fairytales can be enjoyed at bedtime, playtime, or whenever your family has five minutes to spare.

A love of reading and an appreciation of literature is one of the greatest gifts an adult can pass on to a child. Sharing fairytales with even the youngest children brings joy and delight and helps build and strengthen bonds of love, respect and understanding that can last a lifetime.

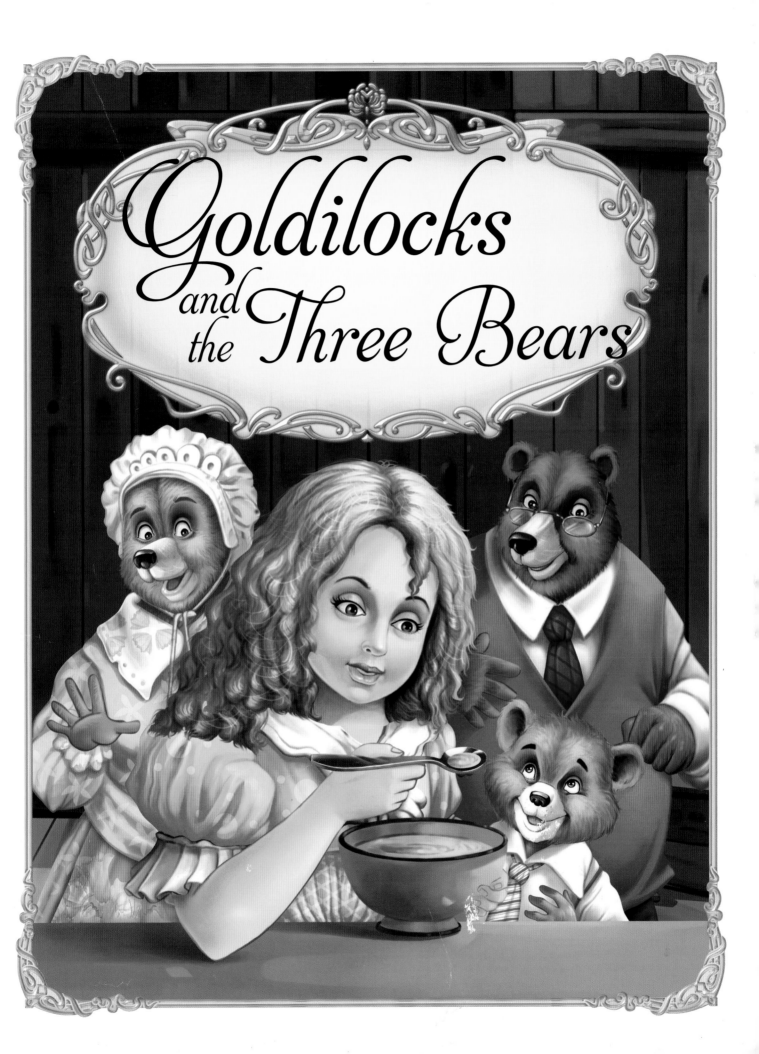

Once upon a time there were three bears who lived together in a house in the woods. One of them was a Father Bear, one was a Mother Bear and the other was a Baby Bear.

They each had a bowl for their porridge: a big bowl for Father Bear, a medium-sized bowl for Mother Bear and a little bowl for Baby Bear. They each had a chair to sit on: a big chair for Father Bear, a medium-sized chair for Mother Bear and a little chair for Baby Bear. And they each had a bed to sleep in: a big bed for Father Bear, a medium-sized bed for Mother Bear and a little bed for Baby Bear.

One day, they made their porridge for breakfast and poured it into the porridge bowls. They decided to go for a walk in the woods while their porridge was cooling so they wouldn't burn their mouths. After all, they were sensible, well-brought-up bears.

While the bears were out walking, a little girl called Goldilocks passed by. She lived on the other side of the woods and had been sent on an errand by her mother. She saw the house and looked in the window. Goldilocks knocked on the door and then bent down and peered in the keyhole. She could see that no one was at home, so she lifted the latch and walked in.

Goldilocks was very pleased when she saw the bowls of porridge sitting on the table. Of course, most people would wait for the bears to come home and hope to be invited to breakfast. However, Goldilocks was rather spoiled and badly brought up, so she set about helping herself.

First she tried Father Bear's porridge, but that was too hot. Next she tried Mother Bear's porridge, but that was too cold. Then she tried Baby Bear's porridge, and that was neither too hot nor too cold. It was just right. Goldilocks liked it so much that she ate it all up.

Then Goldilocks felt tired, so she was pleased when she saw the three chairs. First she tried Father Bear's chair, but that was too hard. Next she tried Mother Bear's chair, but that was too soft. Then she tried Baby Bear's chair, and that was neither too hard nor too soft. It was just right. Goldilocks liked it so much that she sat in it until the chair gave way and she crashed down to the ground. That made her very cross.

Goldilocks was still feeling very tired, so she went upstairs to the bedroom, where she found the three beds. First she tried Father Bear's bed, but that was too hard. Next she tried Mother Bear's bed, but that was too soft. Then she tried Baby Bear's bed, and that was neither too hard nor too soft. It was just right. Goldilocks liked it so much that she pulled the covers over herself and fell fast asleep.

By this time, the three bears thought their porridge would be cool enough and came home to breakfast. When they went to the table, they saw that someone had left the spoons sitting in the porridge.

'Someone has been eating my porridge!' shouted Father Bear.

'Someone has been eating my porridge!' exclaimed Mother Bear.

'Someone has been eating my porridge, and they've eaten it all up!' cried Baby Bear.

The bears realised that somebody had been in their house, so they looked around to see if anything else had been disturbed. When they looked at the chairs, they saw that someone had moved the cushions on the seats around.

'Someone has been sitting in my chair!' shouted Father Bear.

'Someone has been sitting in my chair!' exclaimed Mother Bear.

'Someone has been sitting in my chair, and it's all broken!' cried Baby Bear.

The bears searched further, in case it was a burglar who had been in their house. They went upstairs to their bedroom and saw that the bedclothes on the beds were in disarray.

'Someone has been sleeping in my bed!' shouted Father Bear.

'Someone has been sleeping in my bed!' exclaimed Mother Bear.

'Someone has been sleeping in my bed, and they're still there!' cried Baby Bear.

Goldilocks got a terrible fright when she woke up and saw the three bears standing by the bed, looking at her. She jumped out of the other side of the bed and ran to the open window. She jumped out of the window and landed on the soft, springy grass below. She ran home as fast as she could.

The three bears never saw Goldilocks again, but she learnt her lesson about respecting the belongings of others. And the bears cooked a fresh batch of porridge and had their tasty breakfast!

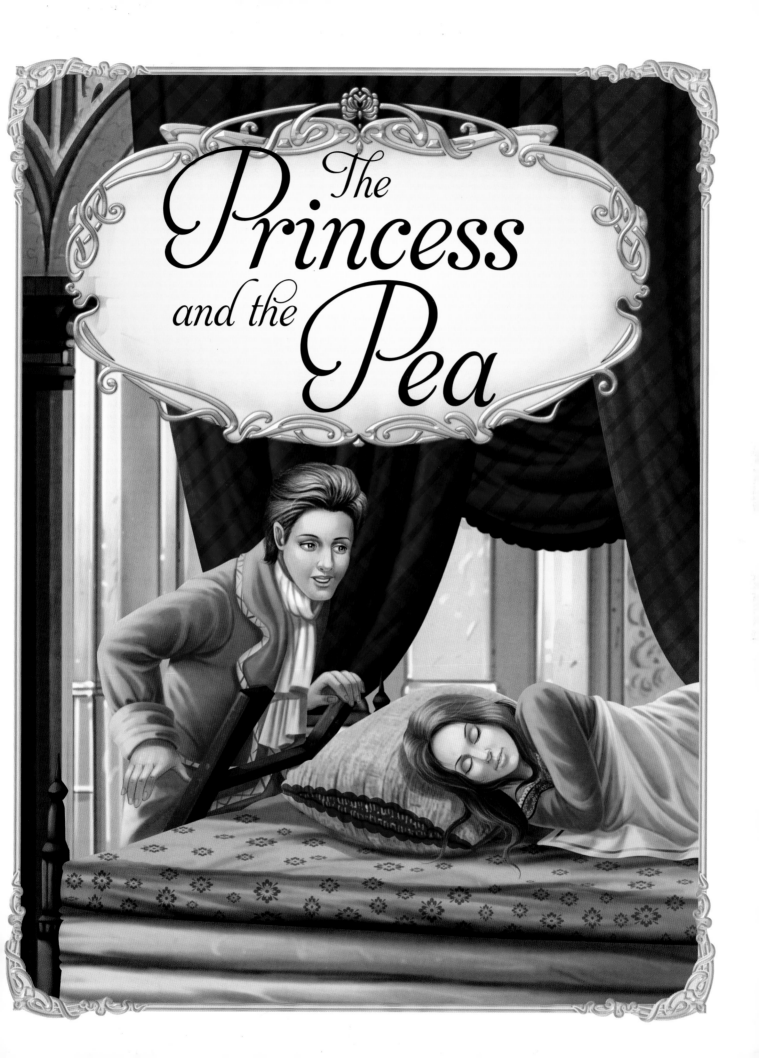

# The Princess and the Pea

There once lived a Prince who wished to marry a Princess. However, she had to be a real Princess.

The Prince travelled all over the world, searching for such a lady, but there was always something wrong. He found Princesses in abundance, but it seemed impossible for him to tell whether they were real Princesses. There always seemed to be something not quite right about the ladies. Finally, the Prince returned home alone to his palace, quite downcast, as he wished so much to have a real Princess for his wife.

One evening, there was a terrible storm. The rain poured down in torrents, lightning cracked across the sky and thunder crashed loudly. It was pitch dark and the wind howled. Suddenly, there was a great knocking at the palace door, and the King, the Prince's father, went to open it.

When he opened the door, the King saw a Princess standing there. The rain and the wind had left her in a sad condition. Her clothes were soaked through and clung to her, and the water trickled down her hair and face. The old King showed the Princess inside and she told him that she was a real Princess.

'Indeed! We'll soon see if that's true!' thought the Prince's mother, the Queen. However, she didn't say a word to anyone about what she was planning to do. She went to the bed in the guest bedroom and rolled the bedclothes and the mattress away. The Queen laid a little pea on the bed frame and replaced the mattress and the bedclothes.

Then the Queen ordered that twenty mattresses be laid one on top of the other over the pea. Next she ordered that twenty feather eiderdowns be laid over the twenty mattresses. This was the bed where the Princess was to sleep.

The next morning, the Queen asked the Princess how she had slept.

'Oh, very badly indeed!' exclaimed the Princess. 'I barely closed my eyes the whole night through. I do not know what was in my bed, but there was definitely something hard underneath me. I am all bruised black and blue. It has hurt me so much!'

Now the Queen knew that this Princess was, indeed, a real Princess because she had felt the pea through twenty mattresses and twenty feather eiderdowns. Only a real Princess could be so delicate and sensitive.

The Prince was overjoyed and married her, for he knew that his wife was a real Princess. As for the pea, it is said that it is kept in the castle in a cabinet of curiosities, where it can still be seen today.

The Royal Pea

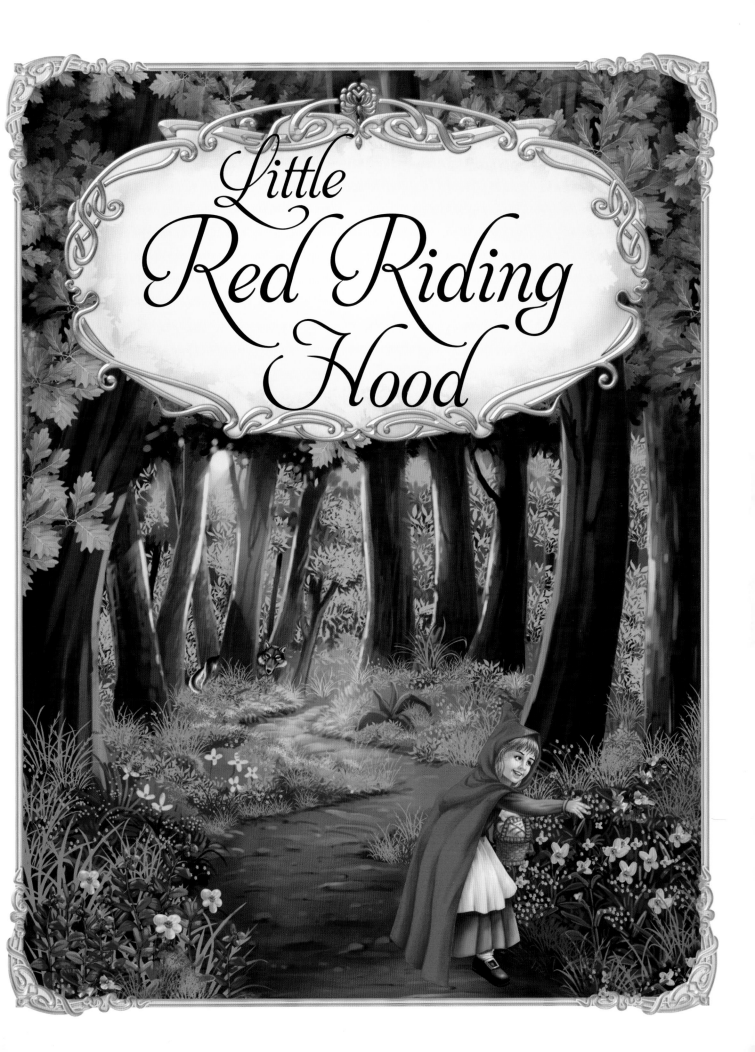

# Little Red Riding Hood

Once upon a time there lived a girl named Little Red Riding Hood. She was called that because she loved to wear a hooded cape of red velvet that her Grandmother had made for her.

One day, her mother said, 'Come Little Red Riding Hood. Your poor Grandmother is ill. I need you to take this bread and cheese to her. Remember, you must stay on the path and go straight there.'

Little Red Riding Hood put the bread and cheese in a basket and set off to her Grandmother's house. Her Grandmother lived on the other side of a nearby wood.

As she was going through the wood, Little Red Riding Hood met a Wolf. The Wolf took one look at Little Red Riding Hood and thought how tasty she looked, but he didn't dare eat her because there were some woodsmen nearby.

'Good day, little maid,' said the Wolf. 'Where are you off to on such a fine day?'

Little Red Riding Hood, who didn't know that it was dangerous to talk to the Wolf, said, 'I am going to see Grandmother. She isn't well, so I am taking her this bread and cheese.'

'Where does she live?' asked the Wolf.

'Why, just through the wood, under the three oak trees,' replied Little Red Riding Hood.

The Wolf thought for a minute, and then said, 'See how pretty the flowers are about here? I am sure your Grandmother would love to see them.'

Little Red Riding Hood looked at the flowers and thought, 'Maybe I should take Grandmother a fresh posy. She'd be so pleased and it is early in the day, so I will still get there in good time.'

'That's a good idea,' said Little Red Riding Hood, and she ran from the path to look for flowers to pick.

Meanwhile, the Wolf ran ahead along the path to Grandmother's house under the three oak trees and knocked on the door.

'Who is there?' asked Grandmother.

'Little Red Riding Hood,' replied the Wolf, imitating her voice, 'with bread and cheese.'

'Come in,' called out Grandmother. 'I am too weak to come to the door.'

The Wolf lifted the latch and went inside. He ate Grandmother in one mouthful. Then he put on a set of her nightclothes and a nightcap, lay down in her bed and drew the curtains so that the room was quite dim.

Little Red Riding Hood gathered a lovely posy of flowers and continued on her way to Grandmother's house. When she got there, she knocked on the door. A husky voice called out, 'Who is there?'

'Little Red Riding Hood, with bread and cheese,' she replied.

'Come in,' called the Wolf. 'I am too weak to come to the door.'

Little Red Riding Hood lifted the latch and went inside. It was quite dark but she could see the shape of her Grandmother under the bedclothes, her nightcap pulled low over her face.

'Put the bread down and come and sit with me,' said the Wolf.

Little Red Riding Hood sat by the bed. She was surprised at how Grandmother looked in her nightclothes.

'Oh Grandmother, what big ears you have!' she said.

'All the better to hear you with,' was the reply.

'Oh Grandmother, what big arms you have!' she said.

'All the better to hug you with,' was the reply.

'Oh Grandmother, what big eyes you have!' she said.

'All the better to see you with,' was the reply.

'Oh Grandmother, what big teeth you have!' she said.

'All the better to eat you with!' was the reply, and the Wolf bounded out of bed and ate Little Red Riding Hood in one mouthful.

The Wolf felt sleepy after his big feast, so he lay down again in the bed and fell asleep. He started to snore very loudly.

Just then, a huntsman who lived nearby was passing the house. 'Goodness, how loudly the old woman is snoring,' he thought. 'She sounds very unwell. I might just pop my head in and see if she is all right.'

The huntsman looked inside and saw the Wolf lying in the bed, fast asleep, his belly full. The huntsman, who had long been hunting the Wolf, took his rifle and was about to shoot when it occurred to him that the Wolf might have eaten the old woman, and she still might be saved.

He took his hunting knife and cut open the Wolf's stomach. Little Red Riding Hood sprang out, saying, 'Oh, it was so dark in there!' Then Grandmother slowly climbed out, shaky but alive.

The huntsman went off with the Wolf's skin and Grandmother and Little Red Riding Hood shared the bread and cheese. 'Never again will I leave the path to run into the woods when my mother has forbidden it,' Little Red Riding Hood thought to herself as she finished her delicious food.

# Thumbelina

There was once a woman who wished to have a child. She went to a fairy, and said, 'I would like to have a child so much. Can you help me?'

'Oh, that is easy,' said the fairy. 'Here is some special barley. Put it into a flower-pot and see what happens.'

The woman went home and planted the barley. Immediately a handsome flower grew, its petals tightly closed like a bud. As the woman watched in astonishment, the flower opened to reveal a graceful little maiden. She was barely half as long as a thumb, so the woman named her Thumbelina. Her bed was a walnut shell with a violet-petal mattress and a rose-petal quilt.

One night, a large, ugly toad crept through the window and saw Thumbelina sleeping in her walnut shell. 'What a pretty little wife for my son,' said the toad, and she took the shell to the stream where she lived with her son.

'We will put her on a water-lily leaf in the middle of the stream so she won't escape,' said the toad to her son. When Thumbelina woke the next morning she began to cry, for she did not know where she was or how to get home.

The old toad swam out to the leaf with her ugly son and said, 'Here is my son. He will be your husband.'

Then they left Thumbelina alone on the water-lily leaf, where she sat and wept. She could not bear to think of life with the ugly toad.

The fish in the stream felt sorry that Thumbelina should have to live with the ugly toads so they surrounded the stalk of the leaf and gnawed it through. The water-lily leaf floated down the stream carrying Thumbelina to faraway lands. Thumbelina was glad, for the toad could not reach her now. She lived by the river and the birds sweetly sang to her.

Summer and autumn passed and then came the long, cold winter. The birds who had sung to her flew away, and the trees and flowers withered. She was dreadfully cold, for her clothes were torn. It began to snow and she shivered with cold and hunger.

One day, while searching for food, Thumbelina came to the cottage of a field-mouse. She knocked on the door.

'You poor little creature,' said the field-mouse when she saw the starving girl. 'Come in and share my dinner.' She quickly came to like Thumbelina and said, 'You can stay with me all winter if you keep my rooms clean.' Thumbelina agreed and was very happy.

'My neighbour is a very rich mole,' said the field-mouse. 'If you had him for a husband you would be well provided for.'

The mole was indeed rich, but he was also quite disagreeable and did not like the sun. The field-mouse insisted Thumbelina sing to him, and the mole fell in love with her sweet voice. He dug a passage from the field-mouse's house to his burrow and encouraged them to visit whenever they liked.

One evening, the mole and Thumbelina were walking together when they came upon a swallow that had died of cold. The mole said, 'How miserable it must be to be a bird! They do nothing but sing in the summer and die of hunger in the winter.'

Thumbelina said nothing. 'Perhaps this bird sang to me sweetly in the summer,' she thought.

That night Thumbelina could not sleep, so she got out of bed and wove a carpet of hay. She carried it to the bird and spread it over him so that he might lie warmly in the cold earth. 'Farewell, pretty bird,' she said.

Thumbelina laid her head on the bird's breast and was surprised when his heart went 'thump, thump'. He was not dead, only numb from the cold and the warm carpet had restored him to life.

The next morning Thumbelina stole out to see him. He was very weak and could barely open an eye to look at her.

'Stay in your warm bed and I will take care of you,' she said. With much care and love Thumbelina nursed him in secret for the whole winter.

When spring came, the swallow bade farewell to Thumbelina. He asked if she would go with him but Thumbelina knew it would make the field-mouse very sad if she left her and said, 'No, I cannot.'

'Farewell then, little maiden,' said the swallow and he flew out into the sunshine.

Soon afterwards, the field-mouse took Thumbelina aside and said, 'You are going to be married to the mole as soon as summer is over.' Thumbelina wept at the thought. Every morning and evening she crept out to see the blue sky. She wished to see her dear swallow again but he had flown far away.

The day approached when the mole was to take Thumbelina away to live with him. She went to say goodbye to the sun. 'Farewell bright sun,' she cried, curling her arm around a red flower. 'Greet the swallow for me, if you should see him again.'

Suddenly she heard a loud 'tweet, tweet!' from above. She looked up and saw the swallow. 'Winter is coming,' he said. 'Now will you fly with me to warmer lands?'

'I will,' said Thumbelina, and she climbed on to the bird's back. The swallow flew over forests and high above mountains, leaving the mole and the field-mouse far behind.

At last they came to a blue lake. Beside it, surrounded by flowers, stood a palace of white marble. The swallow laid Thumbelina gently in a beautiful blossom.

'I live in a nest beneath this castle's tallest turret but you shall live here,' said the swallow with a knowing smile.

On the flower stood a man, as tiny as Thumbelina, wearing a gold crown and delicate wings. A tiny man or woman lived in every flower and he was the King of them all. The little King thought her the prettiest maiden he had ever seen. He asked her to marry him and to be Queen of all the flowers.

Thumbelina happily agreed. For the wedding she was given a lovely pair of wings, which were fastened to her shoulders so she could fly from flower to flower as the little swallow sang a wedding song.

'Farewell, farewell,' said the swallow when it was time to return to the forest for summer.

There he had a nest over the window of a house where a writer of fairytales lived. The swallow sang, 'Tweet, tweet,' and from his song came this story.

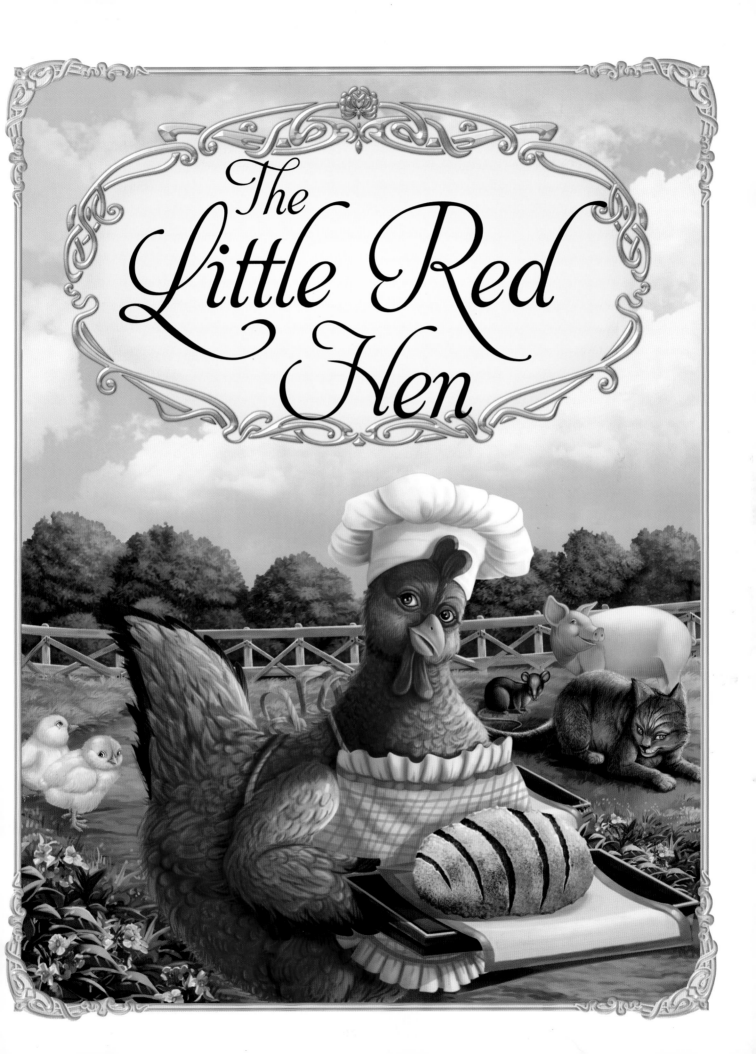

# The Little Red Hen

The Little Red Hen lived in the barnyard with her chicks. She spent her time walking about in her picketty-pecketty way, scratching the ground and looking for worms to feed her family. She loved juicy, fat worms and whenever she found one, she would call out 'Chuck-chuck-chuck!' to her chicks, who would come running. She would share out her find and then it was back to her picketty-pecketty scratching, looking for more.

A Cat usually napped lazily away next to the barn door in the sun, not even bothering to chase the Rat, who ran here and there as he pleased. As for the Pig who lived in the sty, he did not care about anything, as long as he could eat and get fat.

One summer day as she was scratching away, the Little Red Hen found a seed sitting in the dust. She discovered it was a wheat seed. If it was planted, it would grow seeds that could be made into flour and turned into bread.

The Little Red Hen thought of the Cat, who slept all day, and the Rat, who did as he pleased, and the Pig, whose only concern was his food. She called out loudly to them, 'Who will plant this seed?'

But the Cat meowed, 'Not I,' and the Rat squeaked, 'Not I,' and the Pig grunted, 'Not I.'

'Well then,' said the Little Red Hen, 'I will.'

And she did.

Then she went about her duties, scratching for worms in her picketty-pecketty way and feeding her chicks, while the Cat grew fat, and the Rat grew fat, and the Pig grew fat. Meanwhile, the wheat grew tall.

One day, the Little Red Hen decided that the wheat was grown and ripe, ready for harvest. She called out loudly, 'Who will harvest the wheat?'

But the Cat meowed, 'Not I,' and the Rat squeaked, 'Not I,' and the Pig grunted, 'Not I.'

'Well then,' said the Little Red Hen, 'I will.'

And she did.

She went and got the farmer's sickle from his tools in the barn and harvested the wheat in her picketty-pecketty way. The nicely cut wheat lay on the ground, but her little yellow chicks crowded around her, 'peep-peep-peeping' for attention, crying that their mother was neglecting them.

Poor Little Red Hen! She didn't know what to do. She was divided between her duty to her chicks and her duty to the wheat. So, hoping for some help, she called out, 'Who will thresh the wheat?'

But the Cat meowed, 'Not I,' and the Rat squeaked, 'Not I,' and the Pig grunted, 'Not I.'

'Well then,' said the Little Red Hen, 'I will.'

And she did.

Of course, she first went a-hunting worms for her children and made sure that they were all fed and happy. When they were all asleep for their afternoon nap, she went out and threshed the wheat.

Then she called out, 'Who will carry the wheat to the mill to be ground into flour?'

But the Cat meowed, 'Not I,' and the Rat squeaked, 'Not I,' and the Pig grunted, 'Not I.'

'Well then,' said the Little Red Hen, 'I will.'

And she did.

The Little Red Hen loaded up the wheat in a sack and headed off to the mill, far away. The miller ground her wheat into beautiful flour and she trudged back again in her picketty-pecketty way. She even managed, in spite of the load, to catch a juicy worm or two for her chicks. She was so tired when she returned that she went to sleep early.

The Little Red Hen would have loved to sleep late but her chicks woke her, 'peep-peep-peeping' for their breakfast. As she woke, she remembered that today was the day to make the flour into bread. After her children were fed, she went looking for the Cat, the Rat and the Pig. She called out, 'Who will make the bread?'

But the Cat meowed, 'Not I,' and the Rat squeaked, 'Not I,' and the Pig grunted, 'Not I.'

'Well then,' said the Little Red Hen, 'I will.'

And she did.

She put on a fresh apron and a white cook's hat and followed the recipe. She made the dough and kneaded it and shaped it into loaves and put them in the oven to bake.

At last, the bread was ready. A delicious smell wafted across the barnyard. The Cat, the Rat and the Pig all sniffed the air with delight. The Little Red Hen went over to the oven in her picketty-pecketty way. She was very excited about the wonderful bread, which is not surprising, for had she not done all the work?

The Little Red Hen opened the oven and found that the lovely brown loaves of bread were cooked to perfection. Then, out of habit, she called out, 'Who will eat the bread?'

And the Cat meowed, 'I will,' and the Rat squeaked, 'I will,' and the Pig grunted, 'I will.'

But the Little Red Hen said, 'No, you won't. I will.'

And she did!

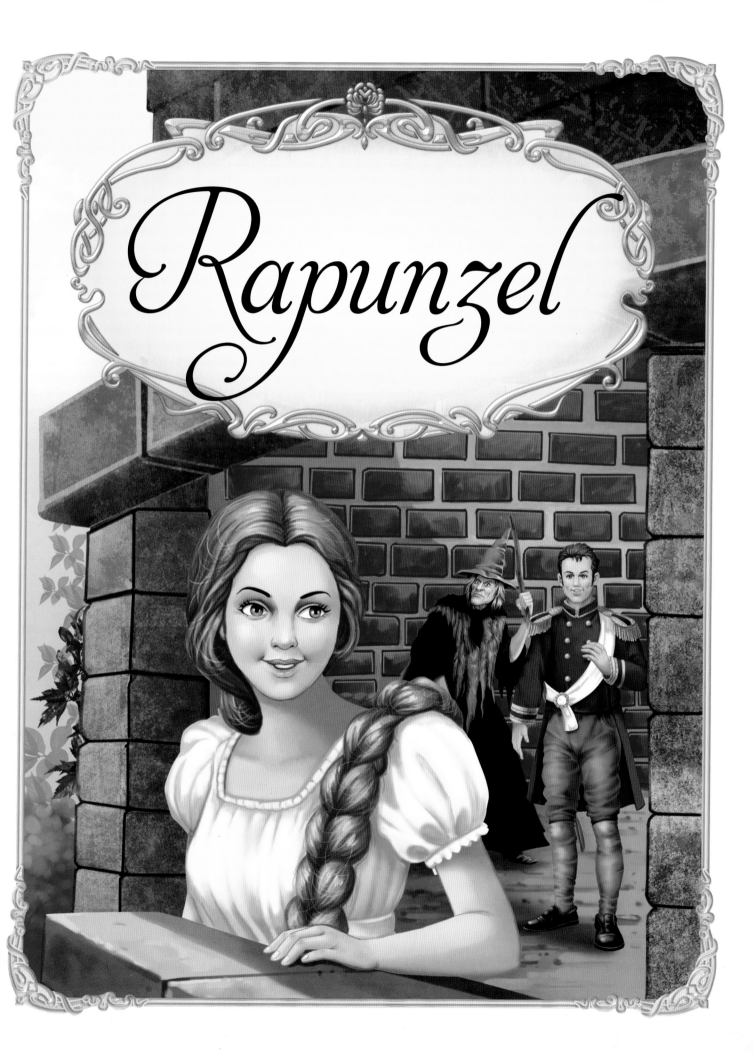

# Rapunzel

Once upon a time there lived a couple who were going to have a child. They had a little window at the back of their house that looked out onto a lovely garden. The garden was surrounded by a high wall and no one dared enter it, for it belonged to a powerful Witch.

One day, the wife stood at the window and saw a garden bed full of the finest lettuce. When she realised she couldn't have any, she pined away and became pale and weak.

'Oh,' she moaned, 'if I can't have some lettuce to eat from the garden, I shall die.'

The man, who loved her dearly, thought, 'I should fetch her some lettuce, no matter what the cost.'

At sunset, the husband climbed over the wall into the Witch's garden. He quickly gathered a handful of lettuce leaves and returned with them to his wife. They tasted so good that her longing for the forbidden food grew stronger than ever. If she were to have any peace of mind, her husband would have to fetch her some more.

When the sun set, he climbed over the wall. Then he drew back in terror, for standing before him was the old Witch.

'How dare you steal my lettuce like a common thief?' she demanded. 'You shall suffer for your foolhardiness!'

'Please, spare me!' he implored. 'My wife saw your lettuce from her window. She had such a desire for it that she would certainly have died if she could not have a taste.'

Then the Witch grew a little less angry. She said, 'If that's so, you may take as much lettuce as you like, but on one condition: you will give me your child when it is born. I will look after it like a mother.' In his terror, the man agreed.

As soon as the child was born, it was taken away by the Witch. She named the girl Rapunzel, which is the name of the lettuce the child's mother so desired. Rapunzel was the most beautiful child under the sun. When she was twelve years old, the Witch shut her up in a tower in the middle of a great wood. The tower had no stairs or doors and only a small window at the very top. When the Witch wanted to get in, she stood under the window and called out:

'Rapunzel, Rapunzel, let down your hair.'

Rapunzel had beautiful, long hair as fine as spun gold. When she heard the Witch calling, she let her braid of hair fall down and the old Witch climbed up it to the top of the tower.

One day, a few years later, a Prince was riding through the wood. As he approached the tower, he heard someone singing so beautifully that he stopped and listened, entranced. It was Rapunzel, who, in her loneliness, passed the time by singing songs, her lovely voice ringing out into the forest.

The Prince longed to see who was singing, but there was no door in the tower. He was so captivated that he returned to the wood every day. One day, he was listening from behind a tree when he saw the old Witch. He heard her call out:

'Rapunzel, Rapunzel, let down your hair.'

Rapunzel let down her hair and the Witch climbed up. 'If that's the way into the tower, I'll try my luck,' thought the Prince.

The next day at sunset, the Prince went to the foot of the tower and cried out:

'Rapunzel, Rapunzel, let down your hair.'

As soon as Rapunzel let it down, the Prince climbed up.

At first Rapunzel was terribly frightened by this young man she had never met before. However, the Prince spoke to her kindly and gently. He told her that his heart had been so touched by her singing that he could not rest until he had met her. Very soon Rapunzel forgot her fear.

The Prince visited her often. When he asked her to marry him, she said, 'I will gladly marry you, only how am I to get out of the tower?' She thought for a moment and said, 'Every time you visit, bring a skein of silk. I will make a ladder. When it is finished, I will climb down and you can take me away on your horse.'

The Prince visited every evening because the Witch came during the day. The Witch knew nothing about this until one day Rapunzel, not thinking, asked the Witch, 'Why are you so much harder to pull up than the Prince? He is always with me in a moment.'

'Wicked child!' cried the Witch. 'I thought I had hidden you from the whole world, yet you have still managed to trick me!'

She grabbed Rapunzel's beautiful hair and picked up a pair of scissors. Snip! Snap! Off it came! The beautiful golden plait lay on the floor. The Witch was so cruel that she sent Rapunzel to a lonely desert to live in misery.

That evening, the Witch fastened the braid of hair to a hook in the window. The Prince came and called out:

'Rapunzel, Rapunzel, let down your hair!'

The Witch threw the plait down, and the Prince climbed up. Instead of his dear Rapunzel, he found the old Witch, laughing mockingly, 'Ha ha! You thought to find a pretty bird but she has flown away and won't sing any more! You will never see her again!'

The Prince was overcome with grief. In his despair, he jumped from the tower. He escaped with his life, but he fell in a thorn bush. The sharp thorns pierced his eyes and he could no longer see.

The Prince wandered, blind and miserable, through the forest. He ate nothing but roots and berries, and wept and mourned the loss of his beloved bride. He wandered like this from place to place for many years, as wretched and unhappy as it was possible to be.

At last, the poor blind Prince wandered to the desert where Rapunzel was living. He was roaming about in despair when he suddenly heard a familiar voice singing. The Prince eagerly followed the lovely sound, and when he was quite close, Rapunzel saw him and recognised him.

Rapunzel threw her arms around the Prince's neck and wept for joy at seeing him again and for sorrow at his poor sightless eyes. But then two of her tears fell into his eyes. Immediately, the Prince's eyes became clear and he could see as well as he had ever done.

The Prince led Rapunzel to his kingdom, where they were received and welcomed with great joy and relief. They were married and lived happily ever after.

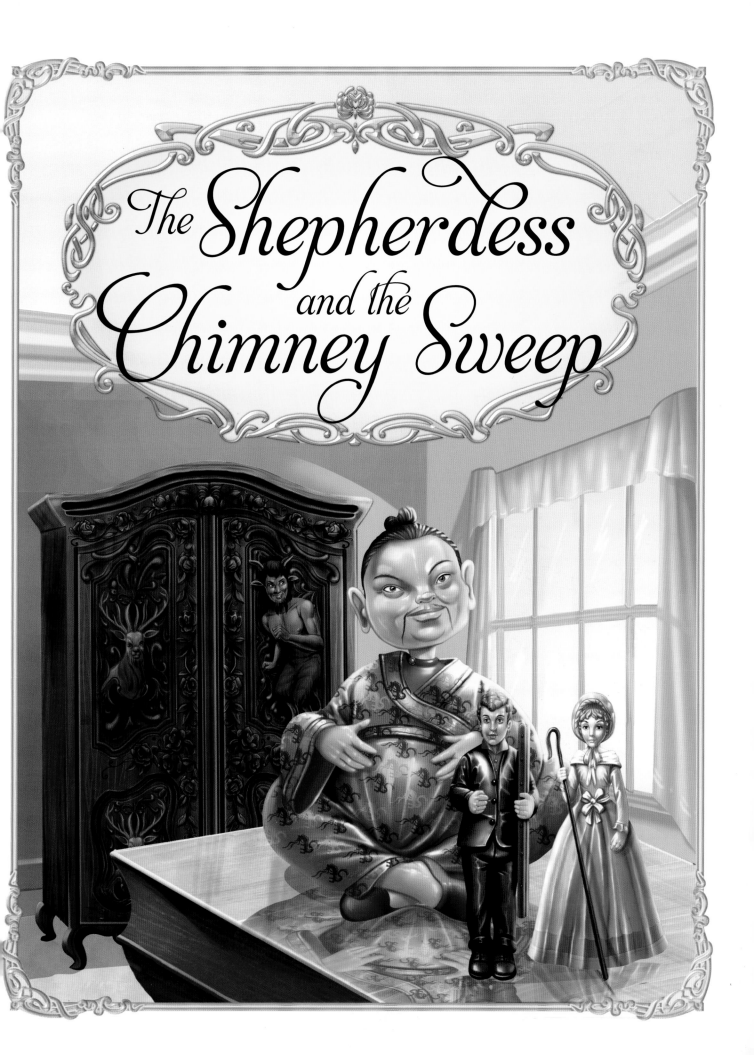

# The Shepherdess
## and the
## Chimney Sweep

Once upon a time in a great big house, there stood an old wooden cupboard, quite black with age. It was covered from top to bottom with carved roses and tulips. Strange scrolls were drawn on it, and in the middle of the scrolls, little stags' heads with antlers peeped out.

In the centre of the cupboard door was the carved figure of a man. He had a wide grin on his face, goat's legs, little horns and a long beard. The children of the house called him 'Major-General-Field-Sergeant-Commander Billy Goat's Legs.' It was a very difficult name to pronounce and there are very few who have ever received such a title, but it seemed incredible how he ever came to be carved at all. Yet there he was.

Major-General-Field-Sergeant-Commander Billy Goat's Legs looked out at a table. On the table stood a very pretty little Shepherdess made of china. She wore a gilded hat and carried a gilded crook and looked very bright and pretty.

Close by her stood a little Chimney Sweep. His dirty clothes were as black as coal and he was also made of china. He held a ladder and his face was fair and rosy. Indeed, that was a mistake by the china makers, as it should have had some dirty marks on it.

The Chimney Sweep and the Shepherdess had been placed side by side. Standing so close, they decided to become engaged to each other. They were very well suited, as they were made of the same sort of china and were equally fragile.

Close by stood an old Chinaman who could nod his head. He was three times as large as they were and was also made of china. He pretended that he was the Shepherdess's grandfather, although he could not prove it. When Major-General-Field-Sergeant-Commander Billy Goat's Legs asked for permission to marry the little Shepherdess, he nodded his head.

'You will have a husband,' said the old Chinaman. 'He has a cupboard full of silver plates, locked up in secret drawers.'

'I won't go into the dark cupboard!' said the little Shepherdess. 'I have heard that he has eleven china wives in there already.'

'You shall be the twelfth,' said the old Chinaman. 'Tonight you shall be married.' And he nodded his head and fell asleep.

The little Shepherdess cried and looked at the china Chimney Sweep. 'I beg you,' she said. 'Go out into the wide world with me, for I cannot stay here.'

'I will do whatever you wish,' said the little Chimney Sweep. 'Let us leave immediately. I can work and look after you.'

'If only we were safely down from the table!' she said. 'I shall not be happy until we are really out in the world.'

The little Chimney Sweep comforted her. He brought his little ladder to help and they managed to reach the floor. When they looked at the cupboard, they saw it was in an uproar. The carved stags pushed out their heads and raised their antlers. Major-General-Field-Sergeant-Commander Billy Goat's Legs cried out, 'They are running away! They are running away!'

The two were frightened, so they jumped into the drawer of the window-seat. In there were several packs of cards and a doll's theatre, where a comedy was being performed. All the queens of hearts, spades, clubs and diamonds sat in the first row, fanning themselves. The play was about two lovers who weren't allowed to marry, and the Shepherdess wept because it reminded her of her own story.

'I cannot bear it,' she said. 'We must get out of the drawer.'

When they reached the floor, they saw the old Chinaman was awake. He shook his whole body until he tipped over and fell down. 'The old Chinaman is coming!' cried the little Shepherdess in fright. 'There is nothing left for us but to go out into the wide world.'

She had her wish. The family had the Chinaman's back mended and a strong rivet put through his neck. He looked as good as new, but he could no longer nod his head.

'Am I to marry her or not?' asked Major-General-Field-Sergeant-Commander Billy Goat's Legs.

The Chimney Sweep and the little Shepherdess looked at the old Chinaman, as they were afraid he might nod, but he couldn't because of the rivet. And so the little china people remained together and were glad of the rivet. They loved each other until they were finally broken into pieces many years later.

When the Chimney Sweep saw that she was quite determined, he said, 'I'll take you through the stove and up the chimney. We shall soon climb too high for anyone to reach us and we'll go through the hole in the top out into the wide world.'

The Chimney Sweep led the Shepherdess to the stove door. 'It looks very dark,' she said in a worried voice. But she found the courage to go in with him.

'Now we are in the chimney,' he said. 'Look, there is a beautiful star shining above us!'

A real star shone down on them, as if it wanted to show them the way. They crept and clambered on. It was frightfully steep but the Chimney Sweep helped the Shepherdess and they climbed higher and higher. At last they reached the top of the chimney.

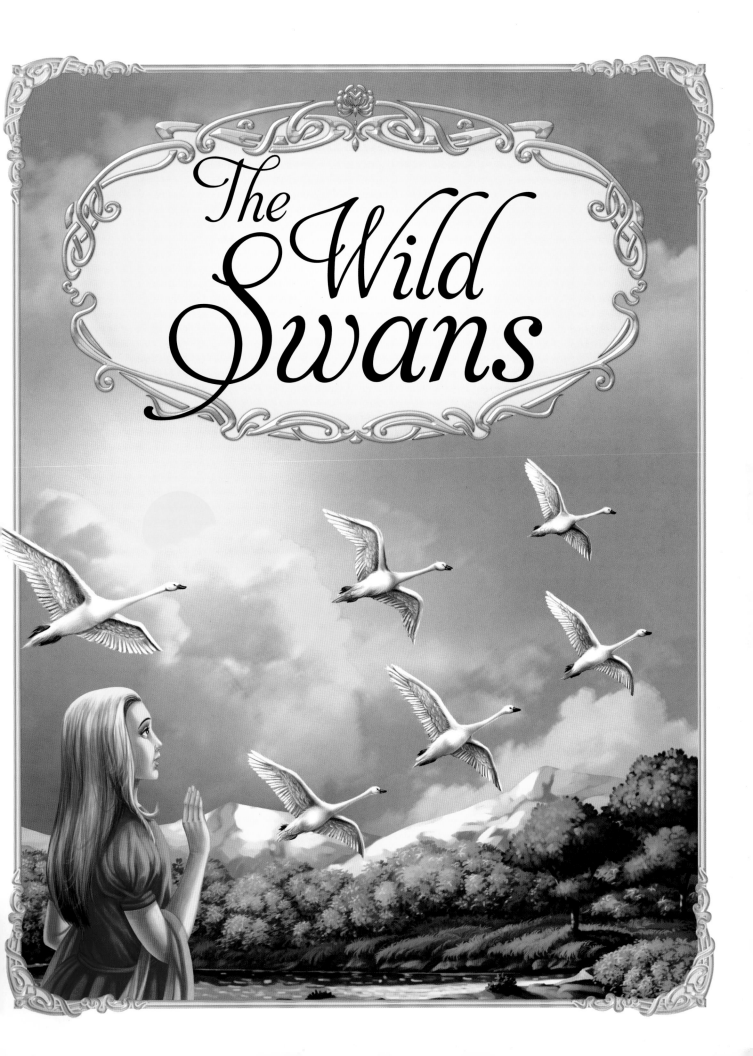

# The Wild Swans

Once upon a time there lived a King. One day he was out hunting in a great wood. When evening came he stopped and realised that he was lost. Suddenly he saw an old woman coming towards him. She was a witch.

'My good woman,' the King said. 'Can you show me the way out of the wood?'

'Yes I can,' she answered. 'But there is one condition. I have a beautiful daughter. Marry her and make her Queen and I will show you the way out.' The King reluctantly agreed.

The old woman led him to her daughter. Although she was very beautiful, the King could not look at her without a feeling of dread. However, he could not break his word, so he helped the maiden on to his horse.

The old woman showed him the way out of the wood and he was soon home at his royal castle, where the wedding was held.

The King's first wife had died, leaving seven children: six boys and one girl, whom he loved more than anything in the world. Afraid their new stepmother might do them some harm, he took the children to live in a lonely castle in the middle of a forest. The road to the castle was hidden so the King used a magic ball of yarn to find it. When he threw it down, it unrolled itself and showed him the way.

The King went so often to see his children that the new Queen grew angry. She wanted to know why he went out alone into the wood so often. She bribed his servants and they told her about the secret castle and the magic ball of yarn.

The Queen did not rest until she had found the yarn. Then she made some white silk shirts with a charm sewn in each of them. When the King was out hunting, she took the shirts into the wood and used the ball of yarn to show her the way to the castle. The children saw someone in the distance but thought it was their father and ran to meet him.

The wicked Queen threw the shirts over the children. When the shirts touched their bodies, they changed into swans and flew away. The Queen went home very pleased, but as the daughter had not run out with her brothers, the Queen knew nothing about her.

The next day the King went to see his children, but he found no one but his daughter.

The girl told him about her brothers turning into swans. The King grieved, but he didn't know that it was his Queen who had done this. He tried to take his daughter back to the royal castle, but she begged the King to let her stay one more night. She thought, 'I must go and look for my brothers.'

When night came, she went into the wood. She ran all night and the next day until she was in another land.

At last she came to a hut with six beds. She crept underneath one and rested on the hard floor. When sunset was near, she saw six swans fly in the window. When they landed, they turned into her brothers.

The boys were delighted to see their sister, but their joy did not last long.

'You can't stay here,' they said. 'This is a robbers' den.'

'Can't you protect me?' asked their sister.

'No,' her brothers answered. 'We are only human every evening for a quarter of an hour.'

Their sister wept and asked, 'Can nothing be done to set you free?'

'No,' they replied. 'It would be too much to ask. For six years you could not speak or laugh. During that time you would have to make six shirts out of nettles. If you spoke before they were finished, the spell would not be broken.' Suddenly, they changed into swans and flew out the window.

The girl decided to set her brothers free, no matter what it cost her. She went out into the wood and climbed a tree and slept there. The next morning, she set to work. She gathered nettles and began sewing them together, not minding the stings. She had no reason to laugh and there was no one to speak to.

A long time passed. One day some huntsmen saw the girl in the tree. 'Who are you?' they called out. But she did not answer.

'Come down!' they cried. 'We won't hurt you.' But she shook her head. The huntsmen climbed the tree, carried her down and brought her to the King of this foreign land.

The King asked kindly, 'Who are you? What were you doing in the tree?'

But she didn't answer.

The King spoke to her in all the languages he knew, but she remained silent. However, the King felt a great love for her. She saw he was very kind and liked him very much. After a few days they were married.

The King had a wicked stepmother who was unhappy with the marriage. 'Who knows where this girl is from?' she asked. 'She doesn't speak a word! She is not worthy of a King!'

After a year had passed, the young Queen had her first child. The King's stepmother stole it away and told the King that his wife had killed it. The King didn't believe her and ordered that no one should harm his wife. All the while, the young Queen went on quietly sewing the nettle shirts.

Some time later, another baby was born. The King's wicked stepmother once again stole the baby and blamed the young Queen, but the King would still not believe her.

When the young Queen had a third baby, the stepmother again stole it away. She accused the young Queen and this time the court forced the King to bring her to justice. She was sentenced to death by fire.

The day she was due to die was the last one of the six years of toil. In that time she had neither spoken nor laughed to free her dear brothers from the evil spell. The six shirts were ready, except one that was missing the right sleeve. The young Queen was led to the pile of wood, carrying the six shirts with her. As the fire was about to be lit, she suddenly shouted out. There were six swans flying towards her and her heart burst with joy.

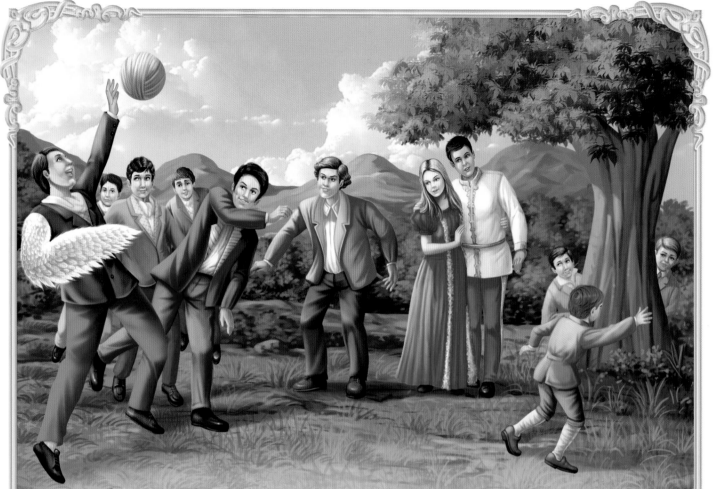

The swans landed around her and stooped so that she could throw the shirts over them. Her brothers stood before her safe and sound. As one shirt was missing the right sleeve, the youngest brother had a swan's wing instead of a left arm.

The young Queen said to the astonished King, 'Dearest husband, now I can speak and tell you that I am innocent.' She told him of the treachery of his stepmother. To their parents' great joy, the three children were found and the wicked stepmother was punished.

The father of the six brothers and young Queen, whose evil wife had died, was brought to them and they celebrated for many days.

The King and young Queen lived many years and grew older with her six brothers in peace and joy.

# The Little Match Girl

It was nearly dark on the last night of the year. It was bitterly cold and the snow was falling fast. In the cold and the dark, a poor little girl roamed through the streets. Her head and feet were bare.

She did have on a pair of slippers when she left home, although they were not much use. They were very large, as they had belonged to her mother. The poor little thing had lost them as she was running across the street, trying to avoid two carriages that were speeding along at a terrible rate. One of the slippers she could not find and the other had been seized by a boy, who ran away with it. So the little girl went on with her naked feet, which were quite red and blue from the cold.

The girl carried a number of matches in her apron pocket and had a bundle of them in her hands. She was a match seller. No one had bought any matches from her the whole day, nor had anyone given her a penny. She crept along, shivering with the cold and hunger, a picture of misery. The snowflakes fell on her long, fair hair, which hung in wet curls on her shoulders, but she ignored them.

Instead, she looked at the lights shining from every window and smelled the delicious aroma of roast goose that hung in the air, for it was New Year's Eve. In a corner between two houses, she sank down and huddled into herself. She pulled her bare feet in underneath her, but she could not keep out the cold.

She dared not go home, for she had not sold any matches and had no money for her family. Besides, it was nearly as cold at home as here, for there was only the roof to cover them. It was full of holes and cracks through which the wind howled, even though they had tried to fill the largest holes with straw and rags.

The Match Girl's hands were almost numb with cold. Oh! A burning match might give her some small comfort, if only she dared to take a single one out of the bundle and strike it against the wall.

She drew a match out of the bundle. 'Scratch!' How it spluttered and blazed as it burned! The flame was warm and bright, like a little candle, as she held her hand over it. It was a wonderful light!

It seemed to the little Match Girl that she was sitting beside a large iron stove, with polished brass feet and a polished chimney. How the fire burned! Her little corner seemed so beautifully snug as the little girl stretched out her feet as though to warm them, when suddenly the little flame went out. The stove vanished and she was left with the remains of the match in her hand.

She struck another match on the wall. It burst into flame brightly. It seemed that where its light fell on the wall, it became as transparent as a veil and she could see into the room. The table was spread with a snow-white tablecloth, on which stood a splendid china dinner set and a steaming roast goose, stuffed with apples and dried plums. And what was even more wonderful was that the goose jumped down from the dish and danced across the room to the little girl.

Then the match went out and there was nothing left but the thick, cold, damp wall in front of her.

She lit another match and found herself sitting under a beautiful Christmas tree. It was even larger and more magnificently decorated than the one that she had seen through the glass door of a rich shopkeeper's house. Thousands of candles burned in the green branches and brightly coloured pictures, like ones she had seen in shop windows, looked down on her. The little girl stretched out her hand to them, and the match went out.

The Christmas lights rose higher until she saw that they were the stars in the sky. Then she saw a star fall, leaving a long trail of fire. 'Someone has just died,' thought the little girl, for her old grandmother, the only person who had ever loved her and who was now no more, had told her that when a star falls, a soul goes up to Heaven.

She struck another match against the wall and the light shone around her. In the brightness stood her old grandmother, bright and radiant, so mild and full of love.

'Grandmother!' she cried out. 'Oh, take me with you! I know you will go away when the match goes out. You will vanish like the warm stove, the roast goose and the magnificent Christmas tree.'

She struck the whole bundle of matches against the wall, for she wished to keep her grandmother there. The matches glowed with a light that was brighter than the sun at noon and her grandmother had never appeared so beautiful and so tall. She took the little girl in her arms and they flew upwards into a place of brightness and joy, where there was neither hunger, nor cold, nor pain.

In the corner in the dawn light, there lay the poor little Match Girl, with pale cheeks and a joyful smile, curled up near the wall. She was still holding the matches in her hand, one bundle of which was burnt.

'She tried to warm herself,' people said. No one could imagine the beautiful things she had seen or understand what splendour she had entered with her grandmother, on that cold New Year's Eve.